Auntie Yang's GREAT SOYBEAN PICNIC

story by Ginnie Lo

illustrations by Beth Lo

Lee & Low Books Inc.
New York

The last part of the trip to Auntie Yang's always took forever. In the backseat of our family's car, my little sister, Pei, and I peered through the window, watching impatiently for the familiar red house to come into view. We hadn't seen our cousins in more than a month.

"Will Ginger and Ping still be awake when we get there?" I asked.

"Don't worry, Jinyi. We'll get to their house before bedtime," Mama replied.

"And Auntie Yang will fix us a delicious snack!" said Baba.

At last we turned down Auntie and Uncle Yang's long, gravel driveway.

"*Dao le, dao le!*" Pei and I shouted. "We're finally here!"

We tumbled out of the car into the humid September night. Crickets chirped noisily as our relatives welcomed us with shouts, laughter, and hugs all around.

Auntie and Uncle Yang lived just outside Chicago, and our family lived a three-hour drive away in a small town in Indiana. Auntie Yang was one of Mama's five sisters. Like Mama and Baba, Auntie and Uncle Yang had come across the ocean to study at universities in the United States. They had all planned to return to their hometowns after graduating, but had stayed because the war in China made it too dangerous to go back.

For a long time Mama was homesick. She missed her family's trips to West Lake, her older brother's stories, her younger brother's tricks, and all her favorite Chinese foods—from simple boiled soybeans to fancy Eight Treasures Rice. There were very few Chinese families in the Midwest back then, so Mama and Auntie Yang made sure our two families visited often. Mama said she wanted us cousins to grow up "as close as four soybeans in a soybean pod."

That weekend in September began like all our visits. On Saturday morning Mama and Auntie Yang made the four of us sit still for Chinese lessons. Afterward Mama helped us with our watercolor paintings, and Auntie Yang showed us how to fold paper into the shapes of boats, monkeys, and rabbits.

In the afternoon the grown-ups continued their endless game of mahjong in the living room while we ran outside to play in the big backyard. I was the leader as we tromped through the high grass with croquet mallets to protect us from any dragons we might meet.

That evening it was my turn to help Auntie Yang and Mama fix dinner. I did my best to fold the pork-and-spinach dumplings into perfectly pleated moon-shaped pieces. I blushed with pride when Auntie Yang complimented me on my work. "Jinyi, you are becoming a very good Chinese cook!" she said.

Soon it was time for dinner. "*Chi fan le!*" Auntie Yang called. "Time to eat!"

As everyone gathered around the table, Auntie Yang ladled steaming boiled dumplings onto our plates. Then the four of us kids had a contest to see who could eat the most. Pei and Ginger each ate six dumplings, and Ping ate seven—but I ate nine dumplings and won the contest!

"Who's ready for a Sunday drive?" Uncle Yang called up the stairs the next morning.

Both families—all eight of us—piled into our family's old car. I got to sit in the front seat between Baba and Uncle Yang, who sang screechy Chinese opera songs as Baba drove. Pei, Ginger, and Ping squeezed together in the back with Mama and Auntie Yang. We passed acres and acres of tall cornstalks. Corn, corn, and more corn.

Suddenly Auntie Yang cried out, "What is that?" She was pointing to a field of leafy green plants. "It looks like *mao dou*," she said. "Soybeans!"

"Couldn't be mao dou!" said Uncle Yang. "This is America, not China."

But it was mao dou. Auntie Yang had discovered a soybean farm tucked in among the cornfields. In Illinois, soybeans were grown to feed cows and pigs, not people—but in China, soybeans were one of the most important foods of all.

Auntie Yang saw a farmer in the soybean field. "Stop the car!" she shouted.

Baba pulled to the side of the road. Auntie quickly hopped out and ran over to the farmer.

"Excuse me, sir. May we pick some of your soybeans?"

"Sure you can. Do you have a little pig at home?" he asked.

Auntie Yang laughed and shook her head.

A few minutes later, she ran back to the car, hugging a huge bundle of soybean plants. Clusters of gray-green pods dangled and swayed from the branches. Quickly, we all climbed out of the car to gather bundles of soybeans from the field. Then we packed them into the trunk. The fuzzy soybean pods tickled my chin and cheeks and made me giggle.

When we got home, Auntie Yang and Mama started heating a huge pot of water on the stove. Then they began to prepare stir-fried dishes to go with the soybeans. Pei, Ginger, Ping, and I piled the soybean plants on the table. We picked off the pods and plunked them into a big yellow bowl.

Once the water began to boil, Auntie Yang added salt and dropped the pods in carefully. In fifteen minutes the soybeans were done. Auntie Yang took her bamboo ladle and scooped some pods into a bowl. Then she and Mama taught us the best way to eat soybeans.

"First, put the whole pod in your mouth, holding the end of it between your fingertips," Auntie instructed. "Then gently close your lips and pull the pod straight out, sucking all the salty juice."

"The soybeans will pop out one by one, all in a row, onto your tongue," Mama said.

"Most soybean pods have three beans, some have two, and a few have only one lonely bean in the pod," Auntie Yang told us.

"But if you get a four-bean pod, you are a lucky Chinese American girl," added Mama.

"And if you happen to get a five-bean pod, well, you are more fortunate than the emperor of China," said Auntie Yang.

The soybeans were still steaming hot when Mama and Auntie Yang called everyone to dinner. Pei, Ginger, Ping, and I helped carry the food outside, and Baba and Uncle Yang joined us at the picnic table.

"Back home," Baba said, "we eat soybeans a thousand different ways: salted, dried, pickled, and fried."

"But we like them best boiled just like this," said Mama with a big smile on her face.

"Soybeans are the greatest discovery in America!" I said, and everyone cheered.

At the end of dinner, our plates were covered with mountains of limp, empty soybean pods piled almost as high as the famous Yellow Mountain in Uncle Yang's hometown province in China.

That was our family's first soybean picnic.

The next summer Auntie Yang talked to the farmer again. "This year I need to pick a few more soybeans. Is that okay?"

"Sure. Did you buy another little pig?"

Auntie Yang just laughed.

That year Auntie Yang invited six Chinese families from around Chicago to come and enjoy our Illinois soybeans. The day of the picnic, the four of us cousins waited outside, watching for the guests to arrive.

By two o'clock in the afternoon, the Chens, Liaos, Chus, Tans, Liangs, and Lius had arrived. Luckily, there were lots of kids just our ages who all spoke Chinese as badly as we did! We ate soybeans with our new Chinese American friends and played outside until dark, when the fireflies came out.

The year after that, word had spread all over Chicago:
SOYBEAN PICNIC AT THE YANGS' HOUSE SATURDAY AFTERNOON!
Auntie Yang went to the farmer again.

"This year I need *a lot* of soybeans to feed my big, big family in Chicago.
We come from China, where soybeans are one of our favorite foods. If we
can have part of your crop, we will pay you for the soybeans."

On Saturday, thirty Chinese families drove up the Yangs' gravel driveway.
Everyone hurried to the farmer's field to pick soybeans. It was hard work,
but we quickly filled a big trailer with mounds of soybean plants.

Back at Auntie and Uncle Yang's house, while the grown-ups set up
picnic tables, we played hide-and-seek and red rover and flew kites with
the other kids.

We couldn't wait for the food to be ready. While the soybeans were cooking, the mothers brought out dozens of delicious Chinese dishes they had prepared earlier. Everything smelled so good! There were steaming platters of Chinese meatballs with cabbage and bean threads, and spicy tofu with ground pork and salted black beans. Pei and I squealed when we saw the whole head of the steamed fish with its cloudy eye staring straight up from the plate.

Finally, everyone sat down to eat. We ate and ate, and ate some more, our chopsticks clicking against the sides of the porcelain rice bowls.

The soybean feast went on late into the night. As the last family drove away, our new friends called out the car window, "Auntie Yang, thank you for a *great* soybean picnic!"

The next day Mama and Auntie Yang sat down together to write their weekly letter to their family in China.

We have made many new Chinese friends in America since we discovered soybeans here! We are not as homesick as we used to be, but we still miss you all very, very much and wish you could come eat soybeans with us in Chicago.

The soybean picnic grew and grew until it was too big to be held in Auntie and Uncle Yang's backyard. Eventually, more than two hundred Chinese mothers, fathers, grandparents, and children gathered at a city park for the annual soybean event. By then Pei, Ginger, Ping, and I were away at college, and some years we could not attend. But the soybean picnic kept on going.

Then one summer Mama and Auntie Yang's dream came true. All their brothers and sisters came from China for their first ever trip to the United States. We watched as the big silver airplane with striped wings rolled slowly to the gate, and we waited eagerly for our aunties and uncles to appear through the doorway.

"*Huan ying, huan ying!*" we shouted when we saw them. "Welcome to Chicago! Welcome to our home."

By now Auntie and Uncle Yang were in their seventies. Although everyone in the older generation had gray hair and Oldest Uncle walked with a cane, they were as funny and noisy together as the four of us cousins were when we were kids. That first night they chattered and laughed for hours. I understood just enough Chinese to recognize the familiar stories Mama used to tell about their trips to West Lake and the tricks that Youngest Uncle used to play.

The next day Auntie Yang made a special trip to buy soybeans from the farmer's son.

Soon all our aunties and uncles were squeezed around Auntie and Uncle Yang's dining-room table, ready to taste American soybeans. Pei, Ginger, Ping, and I crowded around behind them.

Then we started to eat, squeezing the soybeans onto our tongues and sucking the salty pods. *Yummmm!* Pretty soon the mountain of empty soybean pods reached even *higher* than Yellow Mountain.

Suddenly Auntie Yang stood up, waving an extralong soybean pod. Inside, five plump soybeans were cozily lined up in a row.

"Look, look!" she cried. "I'm luckier than the emperor of China."

"You are luckier than the emperor of Chicago too," said Oldest Uncle.

Everyone laughed and shouted.

Mama squeezed my hand. I knew she wasn't homesick anymore. "Jinyi, do you remember the summer Auntie Yang discovered soybeans in Illinois?" she asked.

"I'll never forget it," I said. "But today is Auntie Yang's greatest soybean picnic ever!"

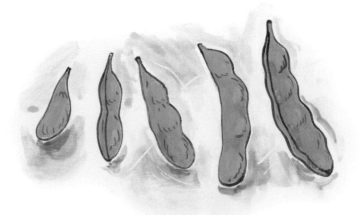

Author's and Illustrator's Note

Auntie Yang, circa 1993

This story of four Chinese American cousins who grew up "as close as four soybeans in a soybean pod" was inspired by our childhood experiences and our special memories of Auntie Yang's soybean picnics.

Beth Lo, cousins Vivian and Ginger Yang, and Ginnie Lo, circa 1957

Auntie Yang was one of our mother's older sisters. In 1945, she and our mother bravely left their family behind in China to attend college overseas. Together they made the long and difficult journey to the United States, where they joined their husbands, who had already moved there to study at American universities. After earning their degrees, our parents moved to Indiana, while the Yangs settled in Illinois.

Picking soybeans in the field (above)

Children lined up at the picnic buffet table (right)

We will never forget the weekend Auntie Yang discovered soybeans near her house. What began as a small, spontaneous picnic for our two families grew into a large annual event. The soybean picnic quickly became an important Chicago area gathering for young Chinese immigrant families who had been displaced by the political upheaval in China during World War II. The picnic continued to grow over a span of forty years and was always one of the highlights of late summer.

Today the fields where we picked soybeans are covered with shopping malls, and we buy frozen soybeans at the supermarket. But our happy memories of Auntie Yang's soybean picnics are with us still. Many a romance began over steaming plates of soybeans, and three generations of families who took part in the tradition remain lifelong friends.

Daddy Lo at the registration table for the fourteenth annual soybean picnic (above)

Guests at the soybean picnic (above right)

Auntie Yang (right)

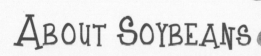

About Soybeans

Soybeans, which are called *mao dou* in Chinese, are also known by the Japanese name *edamame*. They are a staple ingredient in many Asian cuisines. Originally cultivated in northeastern China about five thousand years ago, soybeans arrived in North America in the late 1700s. At first the soybean cargo was not intended to be eaten. It was only used as a weight to balance the sailing ships. Toward the end of the nineteenth century, farmers in the United States began to plant soybeans as feed for their livestock. Today soybeans are a popular food that Americans of many backgrounds enjoy.

Soybeans are extremely nutritious and amazingly versatile. Rich in protein, they are an excellent substitute for meat. There are hundreds of ways soybeans can be consumed—from tofu to soy milk to spicy and sweet sauces. Cooking oil and baking flour are made from soybeans. Soybeans are also used to create industrial products such as ink, fabric, insulation, plastic, and fuel. Today the United States is the world's leading producer of soybeans, shipping millions of tons annually to the leading importer of soybeans: China.

GLOSSARY

This guide provides an explanation of English and Chinese words that may be unfamiliar, including pronunciations for Chinese words that approximate how they are said in Mandarin.

爸 爸 **Baba** (bah-bah): familiar name for father; Papa

bean thread: long, clear noodle made from beans and water

吃 饭 了 **Chi fan le.** (chr fan luh): Time to eat.

到 了 **Dao le.** (dow luh): We're here. *or* We've arrived.

dumpling: very thin, round piece of dough folded over a filling, usually of meat and/or vegetables, pinched closed, and boiled or fried; a popular Chinese food

Eight Treasures Rice: special dessert made with a mound of steamed sticky rice; the sweet "treasures" in the rice are eight different kinds of fruits and seeds

emperor: powerful head ruler of a Chinese dynasty or empire; China was ruled by emperors until 1911

欢 迎 **huan ying** (whan ying): welcome

锦 怡 **Jinyi** (jin-ee): female name meaning "bright and happy"

mahjong: game of Chinese origin usually played by four people with dominolike tiles

毛 豆 **mao dou** (mao doe): soybeans

佩 **Pei** (pay): female name meaning "admire"

平 **Ping** (ping): female name meaning "peace"

Yellow Mountain: famous mountain in the Chinese province of Anhui; also known as Huang Shan

**In loving memory of our aunt Jean Chiaching Yang, 1913–2006
and our uncle Richard Fu Hsien Yang, 1917–2010
—G.L. and B.L.**

Thanks and much love to Mommy and Daddy Lo for our happy childhood memories. Special thanks to cousin Allen Yang for tracking down the old family photographs and to Dr. Jean Yuanpeng Wu, Department of East Asian Languages and Literature, University of Oregon, for editorial assistance.

LEE & LOW BOOKS Inc., 95 Madison Avenue, New York, NY 10016, leeandlow.com
Manufactured in Singapore by Tien Wah Press, September 2012
Book design by David and Susan Neuhaus/NeuStudio. Book production by The Kids at Our House. The text is set in Highlander ITC. The illustrations were created by painting with ceramic underglazes on handmade porcelain plates, which were then fired. Plates photographed by Chris Autio.
10 9 8 7 6 5 4 3 2
First Edition

Library of Congress Cataloging-in-Publication Data
Lo, Ginnie.
Auntie Yang's great soybean picnic / story by Ginnie Lo ; illustrations by Beth Lo.
p. cm.
Summary: "A Chinese American girl's Auntie Yang discovers soybeans—a favorite Chinese food—growing in Illinois, leading her family to a soybean picnic tradition that grows into an annual community event. Includes author's note and glossary"—Provided by publisher.
ISBN 978-1-60060-442-3 (hardcover : alk. paper)
1. Chinese Americans—Juvenile fiction. [1. Chinese Americans—Fiction. 2. Family life—Illinois—Fiction. 3. Soybean—Fiction. 4. Illinois—Fiction.]
I. Lo, Beth, ill. II. Title.
PZ7.L778785Aun 2012   [Fic]—dc23   2011051547